Canadian Pacific Railway Company

The Canadian Pacific Railway

Canadian Pacific Railway Company

The Canadian Pacific Railway

ISBN/EAN: 9783742819796

Manufactured in Europe, USA, Canada, Australia, Japa

Cover: Foto ©Andreas Hilbeck / pixelio.de

Manufactured and distributed by brebook publishing software
(www.brebook.com)

Canadian Pacific Railway Company

The Canadian Pacific Railway

THE

CANADIAN PACIFIC

RAILWAY.

MONTREAL · · ·   · · · 1888.

THE CANADIAN PACIFIC RAILWAY.

RAILWAY from the Atlantic to the Pacific, all the way on British soil, was long the dream of a few in Canada. This dream of the few became, in time, the hope of the many, and on the confederation of the British North American provinces, in 1867, its realization was found to be a political necessity. Then the Government of the new Dominion of Canada set about the building of the Canadian Pacific Railway, a work of such vast proportions that the richest empire of Europe might well have hesitated before entering upon it.

Much of the country through which the railway must be built was unexplored. Towards the east, all about Lake Superior, and beyond to Red River, was a vast rocky region, where Nature in her younger days had run riot, and where deep lakes and mighty rivers in every direction opposed the progress of the engineer. Beyond Red River for a thousand miles stretched a great plain, known only to the wild Indian and the fur trader; then came the mountains, range after range, in close succession, and all unexplored. Through all this, for a distance of nearly three thousand miles, the railway surveys had first to be made. These consumed much time and money; people became impatient and found fault and doubted. There were differences of opinion, and these differences became questions of domestic politics, dividing parties, and it was not until 1875 that the work of construction commenced in earnest.

But the machinery of Government is ill adapted, at best, to the carrying on of such an enterprise, and in this case it was blocked or retarded by political jealousies and party strife. Governments changed and delays occurred, until finally, in 1880, it was decided almost by common consent to surrender the work to a private company.

The explorations and surveys for the railway had made known the character of the country it was to traverse. In the wilderness east, north, and west of Lake Superior, forests of pine and other timber, and mineral deposits of incalculable value, were found, and millions of acres of agricultural land as well. The vast prairie district between Winnipeg and the Rocky Mountains proved to be wonderfully rich in its agricultural resources. Towards the mountains great coal-fields were discovered, and British Columbia, beyond, was known to contain almost every element of traffic and wealth. Thousands of people had settled on the prairies of the Northwest, and their success had brought tens of thousands more. The political reasons for building the railway were lost sight of and commercial reasons took their place, and there was no difficulty in finding a party of capitalists ready and willing to relieve the Government of the work and carry it on as a commercial enterprise. The Canadian Pacific Railway Company was organized early in 1881, and immediately entered into a contract with the Government to complete the line within ten years.

The railway system of Eastern Canada had already advanced far up the Ottawa valley, attracted mainly by the rapidly growing traffic from the pine forests, and it was from a point of connection with this system that the Canadian Pacific Railway had to be carried through to the Pacific coast, a distance of two thousand five hundred and fifty miles. Of this, the Government had under construction one section of four hundred and twenty-five miles between Lake Superior and Winnipeg, and another of two hundred and thirteen miles from Burrard Inlet, on the Pacific coast, eastward to Kamloops Lake in British Columbia. The company undertook the building of the remaining nineteen hundred and twenty miles, and for this it was to receive from the Government a number of valuable privileges and immunities, and twenty-five million dollars in money and twenty-five million acres of agricultural land. The two sections of the railway already under construction were to be finished by the Government, and, together with a branch line of sixty-five miles already in operation from Winnipeg southward to the boundary of the United States, were to be given to the company, in addition to its subsidies in money and lands; and the entire railway when completed was to remain the property of the company.

With these liberal subventions the company set about its task most vigorously. While the engineers were exploring the more difficult and less known section from the Ottawa River to and around Lake Superior, and marking out a line for the navvies, work was commenced at Winnipeg and pushed westward across the prairies, where one hundred and sixty miles of the railway were completed before the end of the first year. During the second year the rails advanced four hundred and fifty miles. The end of the third year found them at the summit of the Rocky Mountains, and the fourth in the Selkirks, nearly a thousand and fifty miles from Winnipeg.

While such rapid progress was being made west of Winnipeg, the rails advancing at an average rate of more than three miles each working day, for months in succession, and sometimes five and even six miles in a day, armies of men with all modern appliances and thousands of tons of dynamite were breaking down the barriers of hard and tough Laurentian and Huronian rocks, and pushing the line through the forests north and east of Lake Superior with such energy that eastern Canada and the Canadian Northwest were united by a continuous railway early in 1885.

The government section from the Pacific coast eastward had meanwhile reached Kamloops Lake, and there the company took up the work and carried it on to a connection with the line advancing westward across the Rockies and the Selkirks. The forces working towards each other met at Craigellachie, in Eagle Pass, in the Gold or Columbian range of mountains, and there, on a wet morning, the 7th of November, 1885, the last rail was laid in the main line of the Canadian Pacific Railway.

The energies of the company had not been confined to the mere fulfilment of its contract with the Government. Much more was done in order that the railway might fully serve its purpose as a commercial enterprise. Independent connections with the Atlantic seaboard were secured by the purchase of lines leading eastward to Montreal and Quebec; branch lines to the chief centres of trade in eastern Canada were provided by purchase and construction, to collect and distribute the traffic of the main line; and other branch lines were built in the Northwest for the development of the great prairies.

The close of 1885 found the company, not yet five years old, in possession of no less than 4,315 miles of railway, including the longest continuous line in the world, extending from Quebec and Montreal all the way across the continent to the Pacific Ocean, a distance of three thousand and fifty miles; and by the midsummer of 1886 all this vast system was fully equipped and fairly working throughout. Villages and towns and even cities followed close upon the heels of the line-builders; the forests were cleared away, the prairie's soil was turned over, mines were opened, and even before the last rail was in place the completed sections were carrying a large and profitable traffic. The touch of this young Giant of the North was felt upon the world's commerce almost before his existence was known; and, not content with the trade of the golden shores of the Pacific from California to Alaska, his arms have already stretched out across that broad ocean and grasped the teas and silks of China and Japan to exchange them for the fabrics of Europe.

With just pride in her work, the greatest perhaps that has ever been accomplished by human hands, Canada presents it to the Empire as her contribution to its power and unity,—a new highway to Britain's possessions in the East, guarded throughout by loyal hearts. But she will not rest with this. Her new iron girdle has given a magnetic impulse to her fields, her mines and her manufactories, and the modest colony of yesterday is to-day an energetic nation, with great plans, and hopes, and aspirations.

AY I not tempt you, kind reader, to leave England for a few short weeks and journey with me across that broad land, the beauties and glories of which have only now been brought within our reach? There will be no hardships to endure, no difficulties to overcome, and no dangers or annoyances whatever. You shall see mighty rivers, vast forests, boundless plains, stupendous mountains and wonders innumerable; and you shall see all in comfort, nay, in luxury. If you are a jaded tourist, sick of Old World scenes and smells, you will find everything here fresh and novel. If you are a sportsman, you will meet with unlimited opportunities and endless variety, and no one shall deny your right to shoot or fish at your own sweet will. If you are a mountain climber, you shall have cliffs and peaks and glaciers worthy of your alpenstock; and if you have lived in India, and tiger hunting has lost its zest, a Rocky Mountain grizzly bear will renew your interest in life.

We may choose between a Montreal and a New York steamship. The former will take us directly up the noble St. Lawrence River to the old and picturesque city of Quebec, the "Gibraltar of America," and the most interesting of all the cities of the New World. Its quaint buildings, crowding along the water's edge and perching on the mountain-side, its massive walls and battlements rising tier upon tier to the famous citadel, crowning the mountain-top and dominating the magnificent landscape for many miles around, plainly tell of a place and a people with a history. All about this ancient stronghold, first of the French and then of the English, every height and hill-side has been the scene of desperately fought battles. Here the French made their last fight for empire in America, in the memorable battle in which Wolfe and Montcalm fell. But peace has prevailed for many years; the fortifications are giving place to warehouses, manufactories, hotels and universities, and the great new docks of massive masonry indicate that Quebec is about to re-enter the contest with Montreal for commercial supremacy in Canada.

Here we find the easternmost extension of the Canadian Pacific Railway, and one of its trains will take us in a few hours along the north bank of the St. Lawrence, through a well-tilled country and a chain of quaint French towns and villages, to Montreal, the commercial capital of the Dominion.

QUEBEC.

Had we chosen a New York steamship our route would have brought us from the American metropolis northward by railway along the banks of the far-famed Hudson River to Albany, and thence through Saratoga and along the shores of Lake George and Lake Champlain to Montreal,—a day or a night from New York.

Here in Montreal, a hundred years before the British conquest of Canada, the French bartered with the Indians, and from here their hardy soldiers, priests, traders and *royageurs* explored the vast wilderness beyond, building forts, establishing missions and trading-posts, and planting settlements on all the great rivers and lakes. From here, until long after the British occupation, the wants of the Indians were supplied in exchange for furs and peltries, and in this trade Montreal grew rich and important.

But finally a change came. The appearance of steam navigation on the inland waters accelerated the settlement of the fertile country at the west, towns and cities sprang up about the old outposts of the missionaries and fur-traders, the Indians receded and disappeared, and agricultural products took the place of furs in the commerce of Montreal. Then came the railways penetrating the interior in every direction, bringing still greater changes and giving

MONTREAL.

a wonderful impetus to the western country, and Montreal grew apace. And now we find it rising from the broad St. Lawrence to the slopes of Mount Royal, and looking out over a densely peopled country dotted with bright and charming villages, — a large and beautiful city, half French, half English, half ancient, half modern; with countless churches, imposing public buildings, magnificent hotels, and tasteful and costly residences; with long lines of massive warehouses, immense grain elevators and many-windowed factories; and with miles of docks crowded with shipping of all descriptions, from the smallest river craft to the largest ocean vessels.

HICHEVER way we came, Montreal should be regarded as the initial point of our transcontinental journey, for it is the principal eastern terminus of the Canadian Pacific Railway, and it is the terminus not only of the main line, but of numerous other lines built and acquired by the company to gather up and distribute its traffic. From here for a thousand miles we have the choice of two routes. We may go through the farms and orchards of Ontario to Toronto, the second city of Canada in importance, much younger than Montreal, but closely following in the extent of its trade and industries, and hoping soon to surpass its older rival in both,—a modern and handsomely built city, where the solidity and culture of the older East is combined with the brightness and eager activity of the newer West. Here, as at Montreal, many railway lines reach out, and on all sides may be seen the evidences of extensive commerce and great prosperity. From here we may in a few hours visit Niagara, and then, resuming our westward journey by one of the Canadian Pacific lines, four hours will bring us to Owen Sound, on Georgian Bay, whence one of the trim Clyde-built steel steamships of the railway company will take us in less than two days across Lake Huron and through the straits of Sault Ste. Marie, where we will be lifted by enormous locks to the level of Lake Superior, and then across this greatest of fresh-water seas to Port Arthur, on Thunder Bay, where the western section of the Canadian Pacific Railway begins.

But you are impatient to see the mountains, and if you will permit me to choose, dear reader, we will start from Montreal by the main line of the railway, and in order that we may miss nothing we will return by the great lakes, and see Toronto and the Falls of Niagara then.

Although the locomotive is hissing, as if impatient for the signal to go, we have yet a few minutes to spare, and if it is agreeable to you, we will look over the train which is to carry us to the Pacific. Next to the engine we find a long post-office van, in which a number of clerks are busily sorting letters and stowing away mail-sacks, then an express or parcels van, and then another, laden with luggage. Following these are two or three bright and cheerful colonist-coaches, with seats which may be transformed into sleeping-bunks at night, and with all sorts of novel contrivances for the comfort of the hardy and good-looking emigrants who have already secured their places for the long journey to the prairies of the Northwest or the valleys of British Columbia. Next we find two or three handsomely fitted coaches for passengers making short trips along the line, and finally come the sleeping-cars, or "Pullmans," in one of which we are to live for some days and nights. The railway carriages to which you are accustomed are dwarfed to meet Old World conditions, but these in our train seem to be proportioned to the length and breadth of the land. Our sleeping-car is unlike the "Pullmans" you have seen in England, being much larger and far more luxurious. With its soft and rich cushions, silken curtains, thick carpets, delicate carvings and beautiful decorations, and with its numberless and ingenious appliances for convenience and comfort (even to the bath-room so dear to the travelling Englishman), it gives us promise of a delightful journey.

We glide out of the Montreal terminus, pass long, low freight sheds and plethoric grain elevators, run along a terrace above the wharves, pass the railway workshops and an extensive cattle depot, and leave the city behind. For a time we are still among the old French settlements, as is evidenced by the pretty cottages and the long and narrow well-tilled farms. There is an air of thrift and comfort everywhere. We have hills and distant mountains on the one hand and the broad and beautiful Ottawa River on the other. Villages are passed in close succession, and soon we are nearing Ottawa, the capital of the Dominion. High up there, on a bold cliff overlooking the river, are the Government Buildings and the Parliament House of the Dominion, with

NOOK IN SLEEPING CAR.

their gothic towers and many pinnacles, making a magnificent group. Away to the left is Rideau Hall, the residence of the Governor General, and stretching far over the heights beyond, the city.

On the broad flats below are acres, perhaps miles, of great square piles of deals, and the cloud that rises beyond comes from the Chaudière Falls, where the whole volume of the Ottawa River "takes a tumble," and is made to furnish power to a host of saw-mills and manufactories.

It is no wonder that you have been so absorbed in the wide stretches of the Ottawa River, since we left the capital behind, that you have quite forgotten it is lunch-time. That white-aproned, white-jacketed boy will bring you sandwiches, coffee, claret and what not.

TORONTO.

We are beyond the French country now; the farms are larger and the modest cottages have given place to farm-houses, many of them of brick and stone and all having a well-to-do air about them. The towns are larger, there are more manufactories and there is more hurry and more noise. At frequent intervals on the river bank are great saw-mills, surrounded by vast piles of lumber. The logs are floated down from the forests on the Ottawa River and its tributaries, and the product is shipped to Europe, to the United States, and everywhere.

PARLIAMENT BUILDINGS, OTTAWA.

Gradually the towns become smaller and the farms more scattered ; the valley contracts and deepens, and we are in the new country. We leave the Ottawa River, and strike across towards Lake Superior. We are surprised at the thriving villages that have already sprung up here and there, and at the number of hardy pioneers who are clearing away the timber and making homes for themselves. At intervals of four or five hours we come to the railway Divisional Stations, where there are workshops, engine-sheds, and quite a collection of neat cottages. At these places we change engines and then move on. It is a long way from the Ottawa to Lake Superior, but the ever-recurring rocky pine-clad hills, pretty lakes, dark forests, glistening streams and cascades, keep our interest alive. We are alert for the sight of a bear, a moose or a deer, and we do not heed the time. Our only regret is that we cannot stop for even an hour to cast a fly in one of the many tempting pools. A dining-car is attached to our train, — a marvel of comfort and convenience, — and we experience a new and delightful sensation in breakfasting and dining at our ease and in luxury, as we fly along through such wonderful scenery.

At Sudbury, a new-looking town planted in the forest, we find a branch line of railway leading off to the straits of Sault Ste. Marie, where it connects with two American lines extending to Duluth, St. Paul and Minneapolis, and beyond ; and here at Sudbury we see long lines of cars laden with copper ore from the deposits near by, which contain hundreds of millions of tons, and we see furnaces building, which are soon to smelt the copper on the spot. We move on through never-ending hills, meadows, forests and lakes, and now, the second morning from Montreal, we catch glimpses of Lake Superior away to our left, and soon we are running along its precipitous shore. On our right are tree-clad mountains. and there are rocks in plenty all about.

For many hours we look out upon the lake, its face just now still and smooth, and dotted here and there with sails or streaked with the black smoke of a steamer. At times we are back from the lake a mile or more, and high above it ; again we are running along the cliffs on the shore as low down as the engineer dared venture. Hour after hour we glide through tunnels and deep rock-cuttings, over immense embankments, bridges and viaducts, everywhere impressed by the extraordinary difficulties that had to be overcome by the men who built the line.

We cross the Nepigon River, famed for its five-pound trout, run down the shore of Thunder Bay and stop at the station at Port Arthur, a thousand miles from Montreal. This place and Fort William, at the mouth of the Kaministiquia River, a short distance further down the bay, constitute together the lake terminus of the western section of the railway.

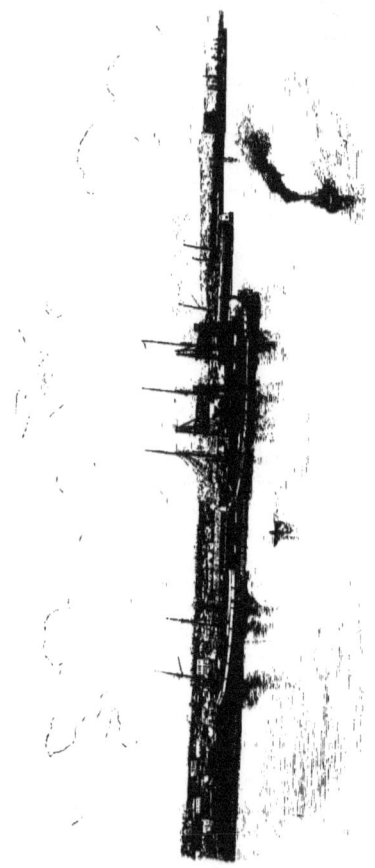

On the way hither we have met numerous long trains laden with grain and flour, cattle and other freight, but we have not until now begun to realize the magnitude of the traffic of the Northwest. Here on every side we see the evidences of it. Long piers and wharves crowded with shipping, great piles of lumber, coal and merchandise, with the railway grain elevators looming above all. One of these elevators at Fort William is a monster, holding twelve hundred thousand bushels. And everything is new,—the creation of a year!

The scenery here is more diversified and beautiful than any we have yet seen. The wide emerald-green waters of Thunder Bay are enclosed by

CABIN OF LAKE STEAMER, CANADIAN PACIFIC LINE.

abrupt black-and-purple basaltic cliffs on the one side, and by hills rising roll upon roll on the other. Here the Kaministiquia River, broad, deep and placid, emerges from a dark forest and joins the waters of Lake Superior, giving little token that but a few miles back it has made a wild plunge from a height exceeding that of Niagara itself.

Our train is increased to provide for the passengers who have come up by steamer and joined us here, and by a goodly number of pleasure-seekers who have been fishing and shooting in the vicinity for a week or two, and who, like ourselves, are bent on seeing the great mountains far to the west. We leave the lake and again move westward, and for a night and part of the following

GRAIN ELEVATOR, FORT WILLIAM, LAKE SUPERIOR.

day we are in a wild, strange country. The rivers seem all in a hurry, and we are seldom out of sight of dancing rapids or foaming cataracts. The deep, rock-bound lakes grow larger as we move westward. Fires have swept through the woods in places and the blackened stumps and the dead trees, with their naked branches stretched out against the sky, are weird and ghost-like as we glide through them in the moonlight. It was through this rough and broken country, for a distance of more than four hundred miles, that Wolseley successfully led his army in 1870 to suppress a rebellion of the half-breeds on Red River, and some of his abandoned boats are yet to be seen from the railway.

But wild and rough as it is this country is full of natural wealth. Valuable minerals and precious metals abound, and from here, mainly, is procured the timber to supply the prairies beyond. As we draw nearer to the prairies, great saw-mills begin to appear, with piles of lumber awaiting shipment; and at all the stations are large accumulations of timber to be moved westward,— firewood, fence-posts, and beams and blocks for all purposes. Many men find employment in these forests, and villages are growing up at intervals. And, strange as it may seem, hardy settlers are clearing the land and making farms in this wilderness; but these are eastern Canadians who were born in the woods, and who despise the cheap ready-made farms of the prairies.

We suddenly emerge from among the trees and enter the wide, level valley of Red River, and in a little while we cross the river on a long iron bridge, catch a glimpse of many strange-looking steamboats, and enter the magic city of Winnipeg.

It will be well worth your while to stop here for a day. Notwithstanding all you have been told about it, you can hardly be prepared to find the frontier trading-post of yesterday transformed into a city of thirty thousand inhabitants, with miles of imposing structures, hotels, stores, banks and theatres, with beautiful churches, schools and colleges, with tasteful and even splendid residences, with immense mills and many manufactories, with a far-reaching trade, and with all the evidences of wealth, comfort and cultivation to be found in cities of a century's growth.

While you will find in Winnipeg the key to much that you will see beyond, you must look beyond for the key to much you will see in Winnipeg. Situated just where the forests end and the vast prairies begin, with thousands of miles of river navigation to the north, south and west, and with railways radiating in every direction like the spokes of a wheel, Winnipeg has become, what it must always be, the commercial focus of the Canadian Northwest. Looking at these long lines of warehouses, filled with goods, and these twenty

RAT PORTAGE, LAKE OF THE WOODS.

miles or more of railway tracks all crowded with cars, you begin to realize the vastness of the country we are about to enter. From here the wants of the people in the west are supplied, and this way come the products of their fields, while from the far north are brought furs in great variety and number.

CITY HALL, WINNIPEG.

ND now for the last stage of our journey. The beautiful sleeping-car in which we came up from Montreal kept on its way westward whilst we were "doing" Winnipeg, but we find another awaiting us, differing from the first only in name. Looking through the train, we find but few of our fellow-passengers of yesterday. Nearly everybody stops at Winnipeg for a longer or shorter time, some to remain permanently, others to visit the land offices of the government or of the Railway Company; others to purchase supplies or materials for their new prairie homes; and still others only to see the town, as we have done. We find among the new passengers representatives of all grades of society, gentlemen travelling for pleasure, sportsmen, merchants and commercial travellers, high-born young men seeking fortunes in large farms or in ranching, sturdy English, Scotch, German and Scandinavian immigrants, land-hunters in plenty, their pockets stuffed with maps and with pamphlets full of land lore, gold and silver miners for the mountains, coal miners for the Saskatchewan country, and professional men of all descriptions. There is not a sorrowful visage in the party; every face wears a bright and expectant look, and the wonderfully clear sky and the brilliant sunshine add to the cheerfulness of the scene.

The Rocky Mountains are yet nearly a thousand miles away. A few short years ago this was a six weeks' journey, under the most favorable circumstances, and it was counted a good trip when the old-time ox-trains, carrying goods and supplies to the distant trading-posts, reached the mountains in three months; but our stages will be numbered by hours instead of days.

Leaving Winnipeg, we strike out at once upon a broad plain as level and green as a billiard table, extending to the north and west apparently without limit, and bordered at the south by a line of trees marking the course of the Assiniboine River. This is not yet the prairie, but a great widening of the valleys of the Red and Assiniboine rivers, which unite at Winnipeg. To the left, and skirting the river, is a continuous line of well-tilled farms, with comfortable farm-houses peering out from among the trees. To the right is a vast meadow, with countless cattle half hidden in the grass. The railway stretches away before us without a curve or deflection as far as the eye can reach, and the motion of the train is hardly felt as we fly along.

As we proceed westward, we imperceptibly reach higher ground, and the country is checkered with fields of grain, and dotted far into the distance with farm-houses and grain-stacks.

Fifty-five miles from Winnipeg we reach Portage la Prairie, another city of a day's growth, and the centre of a well-developed and prosperous farming region. Its big grain elevators and flour mills, its busy streets and substantial houses tell their own story. From here a new railway reaches away two hundred miles to the northwest, making more lands accessible (if more be needed), bringing down grain and cattle, and before long to bring salt and petroleum as well.

Crossing a low range of sand-hills, marking the shore of an ancient lake, we pass through a beautifully undulating country, fertile and well settled, as the busy little towns and the ever-present grain elevators bear evidence.

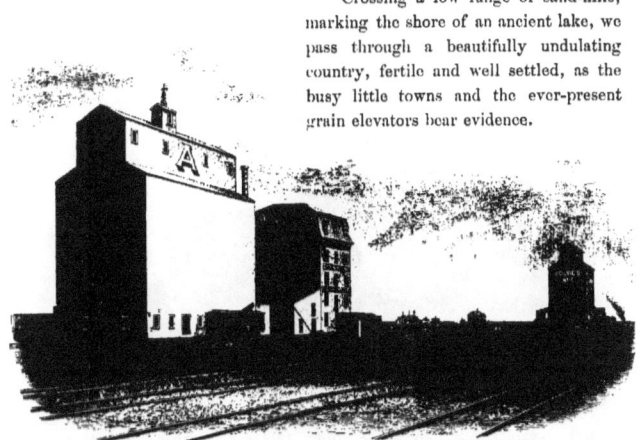

GRAIN ELEVATORS AND FLOUR MILL, PORTAGE LA PRAIRIE, MANITOBA.

One hundred and thirty miles from Winnipeg we cross the Assiniboine River, and reach Brandon, next to Winnipeg the largest town in the Canadian Northwest, a city in fact, although but five years old, with handsome buildings, well-made streets, and an unusual number of large grain elevators and mills.

Leaving Brandon we have fairly reached the first of the great prairie *steppes*, that rise one after the other at long intervals to the Rocky Mountains ; and now we are on the real prairie, not the monotonous, uninteresting plain

your imagination has pictured, but a great billowy ocean of grass and flowers,
now swelling into low hills, again dropping into broad basins with gleaming
ponds, and broken here and there by valleys and by irregular lines of trees
marking the water-courses. The horizon only limits the view ; and, as far as
the eye can reach, the prairie is dotted with newly-made farms, with great
black squares where the sod has just been turned by the plough, and with
herds of cattle. The short, sweet grass, studded with brilliant flowers, covers
the land as with a carpet, ever changing in colour as the flowers of the different seasons and places give to it their predominating hue.

The deep black soil of the valley we left in the morning has given place
to a soil of lighter colour, overlying a porous clay, less inviting to the inex-
perienced agriculturist, but nevertheless of the very highest value, for here
is produced, in the greatest perfection, the most famous of all varieties of
wheat—that known as the "Hard
Fyfe wheat of Manitoba,"—and oats
as well, and rye, barley and flax, and

A PRAIRIE STATION.

gigantic potatoes, and almost everything that can be grown in a temperate
climate. All these flourish here without appreciable drain upon the soil.
Once here, the English farmer soon forgets all about fertilizers. His children
may have to look to such things, but he will not.

We pass station after station, nearly all alike, except as to the size of the
villages surrounding them, some of which are of considerable importance.
The railway buildings at these stations are uniform, and consist of an attractive
station-house for passengers and goods, a great round water-tank, cottages for
the section-men, and the never-ending grain elevators — tall solid structures,
always telling the same story. Every minute or two we see coveys of

"prairie chickens" (pinnated grouse) rising from the grass, startled by the passing train. Ducks of many kinds are seen about the frequent ponds, together with wild geese and cranes, and occasionally great white pelicans. The sportsmen have nearly all dropped off at the different stations. Those who remain are after larger game farther west,—antelope or caribou.

Three hundred miles from Winnipeg we pass through the famous Bell farm, embracing one hundred square miles of land. This is a veritable manufactory of wheat, where the work is done with an almost military organization, ploughing by brigades and reaping by divisions. Think of a farm where the furrows are ordinarily four miles long, and of a country where such a thing is possible ! There are neat stone cottages and ample barns for miles around, and the collection of buildings about the headquarters near the railway station makes a respectable village, there being among them a church, a hotel, a flour-mill, and, of course, a grain elevator, for in this country these elevators appear wherever there is wheat to be handled or stored.

Soon we reach Regina, the capital of the Province of Assiniboia, situated in the centre of an apparently boundless, but very fertile plain. The buildings here have

SMOKING-ROOM IN SLEEPING CAR.

more of a frontier look than those of the larger towns we have left behind ; but it is a busy place, an important centre of trade, and one of the cities of the future. From here a railway branches off to the north, and is pushing away towards Battleford and Edmonton. As we leave the station going westward, we see on our right the Governor's residence, and a little beyond, the headquarters of the Northwest Mounted Police, a body of men of whom Canada is justly proud. This organization is composed of young

SOUTH SASKATCHEWAN RIVER, MEDICINE HAT, ASSINIBOIA.

and picked men, thoroughly drilled, and governed by the strictest military dis cipline. Their firm and considerate rule won the respect and obedience of the Indians long before the advent of the railway, and its coming was attended by none of the lawlessness and violence which have darkly marked the open- ing of new districts elsewhere in America, so wholesome was the fame of these red-coated guardians of the wide prairies.

Leaving Regina we soon pass Moosejaw, four hundred miles from Winni- peg, and commence the ascent of another prairie *steppe*.

We have now nearly reached the end of the continuous settlement, and beyond to the mountains we shall only find the pioneer farmers in groups here and there. The country, while retaining the chief characteristics of the prairie, becomes more broken, and numerous lakes and ponds occur in the depressions. We shall see no trees now for a hundred miles, and without them the short buffalo-grass gives the country a desolate, barren look; but it is far from barren, as the occasional farms testify through their wonder- ful growth of cereals and vegetables. There is a flutter of excitement among the passengers, and a rush to the windows. Antelope! We shall see them often enough now. At Chaplin, we come to one of the Old Wives' lakes, which are extensive bodies of water having no outlet, and consequently alkaline.

We are now entering a very paradise for sportsmen. The lakes become more frequent. Some are salt, some are alkaline, but most of them are clear and fresh. Wild geese, cranes, ducks, — a dozen varieties, — snipe, plover and curlew, all common enough throughout the prairies, are found here in myriads. Water-fowl blacken the surface of the lakes and ponds, long white lines of peli- cans disport themselves along the shores, and we hear the notes and cries of many strange birds whose names I cannot tell you. "Prairie chickens" are abundant on the high ground, and antelope are common in the hills.

The country is reticulated with buffalo trails, and pitted with their wal- lows. A buffalo is a rare sight now, and the last one will soon have disap- peared; but the hope of seeing one keeps all eyes straining. Hour after hour we roll along, with little change in the aspect of the country. The geese and ducks have ceased to interest us, and even a coyote no longer attracts atten- tion; but the beautiful antelope has never-ending charms for us, and as, startled by our approach, he bounds away, we watch the white tuft which serves him for a tail until it disappears in the distance.

We have crossed the high broken country, known here as the Coteau, and far away to the southwest we see the Cypress Hills appearing as a deep blue

ROCKY MOUNTAINS, NEAR CANMORE.

lir.e, and, for want of anything else, we watch these gradually rising as we draw near to them. The railway skirts their base for many miles, following what seems to be a broad valley, and crossing many clear little streams making their way from the hills northward to the Saskatchewan. At Maple Creek, a little town with extensive yards for the shipment of cattle some of which are driven here from Montana, feeding and fattening on the way, we see the red coats of the mounted police who are looking after a large encampment of Indians near by. The Indians are represented on the station platform by braves of high and low degree, squaws and papooses, mostly bent on trading pipes and trinkets for tobacco and silver; a picturesque looking lot, but dirty withal. Leaving the station we catch sight of their encampment a mile or so away, tall, conical "tepees" of well-smoked cloths or skins; Indians in blankets of brilliant colours; hundreds of ponies feeding in the rich grasses; a line of graceful trees in the background, seemingly more beautiful than ever because of their rarity; —all making, with the dark Cypress Hills rising in the distance, a picture most novel and striking.

Two hours later we descend to the valley of the South Saskatchewan and soon arrive at Medicine Hat, a finely situated and rapidly growing town, a thousand miles from Lake Superior. Hereabouts are extensive coal mines from which came the coals we saw moving eastward on the railway; and from near this place a railway extends to other coal mines more than a hundred miles to the southwest. The broad and beautiful Saskatchewan River affords steamboat navigation a long way above, and for a thousand miles or more below; and western enterprise has been quick to seize upon the advantages offered here.

Crossing the river on a long iron bridge, we ascend again to the high prairie, now a rich pasture dotted with lakelets. Everywhere the flower-sprinkled sward is marked by the deep narrow trails of the buffalo, and the saucer-like hollows where the shaggy monsters used to wallow; and strewing the plain in all directions are the whitened skulls of these noble animals now so nearly extinct. There are farms around many of the little stations even so far west as this, and the herds of cattle grazing on the knolls indicate the "ranch country."

As we approach Crowfoot station all are alive for the first view of the Rocky Mountains, yet more than a hundred miles away; and soon we see them, —a glorious line of snowy peaks rising straight from the plain and extending the whole length of the western horizon, seemingly an impenetrable barrier. As we speed on, peak rises behind peak, then dark bands of forest that reach

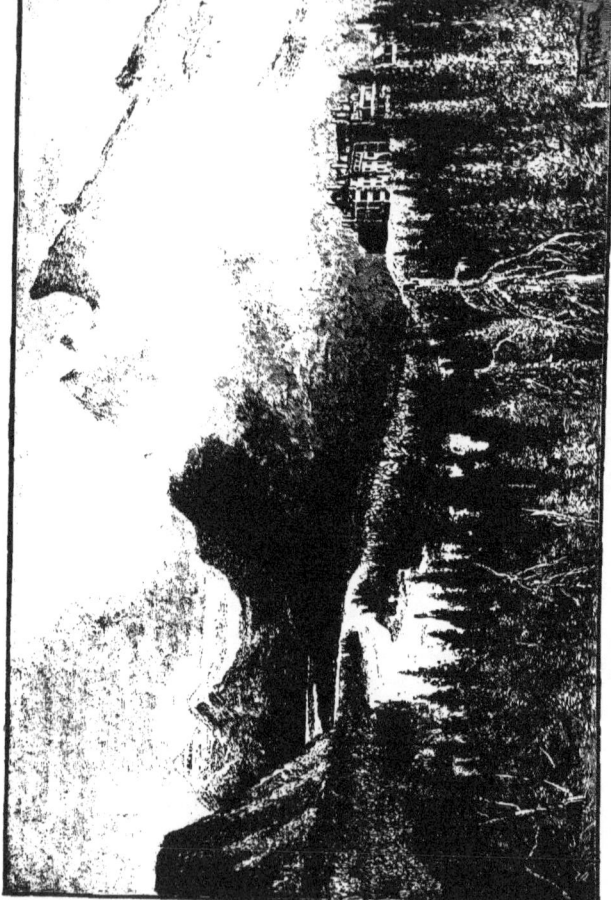

BANFF SPRINGS HOTEL, CANADIAN NATIONAL PARK, ROCKY MOUNTAINS.

up to the snow-line come into view ; the snow-fields and glaciers glisten in the sunlight, and over the rolling tops of the foothills the passes are seen, cleft deep into the heart of the mountains. We are now in the country of the once dreaded Blackfeet, the most handsome and warlike of all the Indian tribes, but now peacefully settled on a reservation near by. We have been running parallel to the tree-lined banks of the Bow River, and now, crossing its crystal waters, we find ourselves on a beautiful hill-girt plateau in the centre of which stands the new city of Calgary, at the base of the Rocky Mountains, 2,262 miles from Montreal and 3,416 feet above the ocean.

Before us, and on either side, the mountains rise in varied forms and in endless change of aspect, as the lights and shadows play upon them. Behind us is the great sea of open prairie. Northward is the wooded district of Edmonton and the North Saskatchewan, full of moose, elk, bear, and all manner of fur-bearing animals and winged game. Southward, stretching away 150 miles to the United States boundary, is the Ranch Country.

You may be sure of a cordial welcome should you visit the ranchmen, and it will be worth your while to do so. You will find them all along the foot-hills, their countless herds feeding far out on the plain. Cattle and horses graze at will all over the country, summer and winter alike. The warm "Chinook" winds from across the mountains keep the ground free from snow in the winter, except for a day or two at a time, and the nutritious and naturally cured grasses are always within reach of the cattle. In the spring and autumn all the ranchmen join in a "round up," to collect and sort out the animals according to the brands of the different owners ; and then the "cow-boy" appears in all his glory. To see these splendid riders "cutting out" or separating the animals from the common herd, lassoing and throwing them, that they may be branded with the owner's mark, or herding a band of free-born and unbroken horses, is well worth coming all this way. The ranchmen, fine fellows from the best families in the East and in England, live here in a lordly way. Admirable horsemen, with abundant leisure and unlimited opportunities for sport, their intense love for this country is no matter of wonder, nor is it surprising that every day brings more young men of the best class to join in this free and joyous life.

All along the base of the mountains clear streams come down to the plain at frequent intervals ; coal crops out on the water-courses, and there is timber in plenty throughout the foothills. The soil is rich and deep, and the climate matchless. What more can one desire?

Leaving Calgary and going westward again, following up the valley of

MOUNT STEPHEN, NEAR THE SUMMIT OF THE ROCKIES.

the Bow, the gradually increasing river terraces and the rounded grassy foot-hills, on which innumerable horses, cattle and sheep are feeding, shut out the mountains for an hour or two.   Suddenly we come upon them grand and stern and close at hand.   For more than six hundred miles and until we reach the Pacific they will be constantly with us.   We enter an almost hidden portal, and find ourselves in a valley between two great mountain ranges.   At every turn of the valley, which is an alternation of precipitous gorges and wide parks, a new picture presents itself.   The beautiful river now roars through a narrow defile, now spreads out into a placid lake, reflecting the forests, cliffs and snowy summits.   Serrated peaks, and vast pyramids of rock with curiously contorted and folded strata, are followed by gigantic castellated masses down whose sides cascades fall thousands of feet.   The marvellous clearness of the air brings out the minutest detail of this Titanic sculpture.   Through the gorges we catch glimpses of glaciers and other strange and rare sights, and now and then of wild goats and mountain sheep, grazing on the cliffs far above us near the snow line.   The mountains would be oppressive in their grandeur, their solemnity and their solitude, but for an occasional mining town or a sportsman's tent, which give a human interest to the scene.

Three hours after leaving Calgary we pass the famous anthracite mines near the base of Cascade Mountain, and soon after stop at the station at Banff, already famous for its hot and sulphurous springs, which possess wonderful curative powers, and which have already attracted thousands of people, many of them from great distances.   The district for miles about has been reserved by the Canadian government as a national park, and much has already been done to add to its natural beauty, or rather, to make its beauties accessi-ble; for in this supremely beautiful place, the hands of man can add but little. Everybody stops here for a day or two at least, and we should do likewise. We will find luxurious quarters in a large and handsomely appointed hotel, perched on a hill overlooking the beautiful valley of Bow River.   The river comes down from its glacier sources at the west, plunges over a precipice beneath the hotel balconies, and, stretching away through the deep, forested valley, disappears among the distant mountains at the east.   Half a dozen ranges of magnificent snow-tipped mountains centre here, each differing from the others in form and colour; and the converging valleys separating them afford matchless views in all directions.   Well-made carriage roads and bridle paths lead to the different springs and wind about among the mountains every-where.

Resuming our journey, we are soon reminded by the increasing nearness of

MOUNT STEPHEN HOUSE—FIELD, ROCKY MOUNTAINS.

the fields of snow and ice on the mountain-slopes that we are reaching a great elevation, and an hour from Banff our train stops at a little station, and we are told that this is the summit of the Rocky Mountains, just a mile above the sea, but it is the summit only in an engineering sense, for the mountains still lift their white heads five thousand to seven thousand feet above us, and stretch away to the northwest and the southeast like a great back-bone, as indeed they are,—the "backbone of the continent."

Two little streams begin here almost from a common source. The waters of one find their way down to the Saskatchewan and into Hudson's Bay and the other joins the flood which the Columbia pours into the Pacific Ocean. Passing three emerald lakes, deep set in the mountains, we follow the west-bound stream down through a tortuous rock-ribbed cañon, where the waters are dashed to foam in incessant leaps and whirls. This is the Wapta or Kicking-Horse pass. Ten miles below the summit we round the base of Mount Stephen, a stupendous mountain rising directly from the railway to a height of more than eight thousand feet, holding on one of its shoulders, and almost over our heads, a glacier whose shining green ice, five hundred feet thick, is slowly crowded over a sheer precipice of dizzy height, and crushed to atoms below. From the railway, clinging to the mountain side, we look down upon the river valley, which, suddenly widening, here holds between the dark pine-clad mountains a mirror-like sheet of water, reflecting with startling fidelity each peak and precipice.

Still following the river, now crossing deep ravines, now piercing projecting rocky spurs, now quietly gliding through level park-like expanses of greensward, with beautiful trees, pretty lakelets and babbling brooks, we soon enter a tremendous gorge whose frowning walls, thousands of feet high, seem to overhang the boiling stream which frets and roars at their base, and this we follow for miles, half shut in from the daylight.

Two hours from the summit and three thousand feet below it, the gorge suddenly expands, and we see before us high up against the sky a jagged line of snowy peaks of new forms and colours. A wide, deep, forest-covered valley intervenes, holding a broad and rapid river. This is the Columbia. The new mountains before us are the Selkirks, and we have now crossed the Rockies. Sweeping round into the Columbia valley we have a glorious mountain view. To the north and south, as far as the eye can reach, we have the Rockies on the one hand and the Selkirks on the other, widely differing in aspect, but each indescribably grand. Both rise from the river in a succession of tree-clad benches, and soon leaving the trees behind, shoot upwards to the regions of

GREAT GLACIER AND GLACIER HOUSE, SELKIRK MOUNTAINS.

perpetual snow and ice. The railway turns down the Columbia, following one of the river-benches through gigantic trees for twenty miles to Donald, where a number of our fellow-passengers leave us. Some of them are miners or prospectors bound for the silver mines in the vicinity, or the gold " diggins " further down the river; others are ambitious sportsmen, who are seeking caribou or mountain sheep — the famous "big horns." They will not fail to run upon a bear now and then, black or cinnamon, and perchance a grizzly.

Crossing the Columbia, and following it down through a great cañon, through tunnels and deep rock-cuttings, we shortly enter the Beaver valley and commence the ascent of the Selkirks, and then for twenty miles we

DINING-ROOM—GLACIER HOUSE.

climb along the mountain sides, through dense forests of enormous trees, until, near the summit, we find ourselves in the midst of a wonderful group of peaks of fantastic shapes and many colours. At the summit itself, four thousand five hundred feet above tide-water, is a natural resting-place, — a broad level area surrounded by mountain monarchs, all of them in the deadly embrace of glaciers. Strange, under this warm summer's sky, to see this battle going on between rocks and ice — a battle begun æons ago and to continue for æons to come ! To the north, and so near us that we imagine that we hear the crackling of the ice, is a great glacier whose clear green fissures we can plainly see. To the south is another, vastly larger, by the

THE GREAT GLACIER OF THE SELKIRKS.

side of which the greatest of those of the Alps would be insignificant. Smaller glaciers find lodgment on all the mountain benches and slopes, whence innumerable sparkling cascades of icy water come leaping down.

Descending westerly from the summit we reach in a few minutes the Glacier House, a delightful hotel situated almost in the face of the Great Glacier and at the foot of the grandest of all the peaks of the Selkirks, — Sir Donald, — an acute pyramid of naked rock shooting up nearly eight thousand feet above us. In the dark valley far below we see the glacier-fed Illicilliwaet glistening through the tree-tops, and beyond and everywhere the mountains rise in majesty and immensity beyond all comparison. To reach the deep valley below, the engineers wound the railway in a series of great curves or loops all about the mountain slopes, and as we move on this marvellous scene is presented to us in every aspect. We plunge again for hours through precipitous gorges, deep and dark, and again cross the Columbia River, which has made a great detour around the Selkirk Mountains while we have come directly through them. The river is wider and deeper here, and navigable by steamboats southward for nearly two hundred miles.

We are now confronted by the Gold range, another grand snow-clad series of mountains, but broken directly across, and offering no obstacle to the railway. The deep and narrow pass through this range takes us for forty miles or more between parallel lines of almost vertical cliffs, into the faces of which the line is frequently crowded by deep black lakes; and all the way the bottom of the valley is thickly set with trees of many varieties and astonishing size, exceeding even those of the Columbia.

A sudden flash of light indicates that we have emerged from the pass, and we see stretching away before us the Shuswap lakes, whose crystal waters are hemmed and broken in every way by abruptly rising mountains. After playing hide-and-seek with these lovely lakes for an hour or two, the valley of the South Thompson River is reached — a wide almost treeless valley, already occupied from end to end by farms and cattle ranches ; and here for the first time irrigating ditches appear. Flocks and herds are grazing everywhere, and the ever present mountains look down upon us more kindly than has been their wont.

The railway passes Kamloops Lake, shooting through tunnel after tunnel, and then the valley shuts in and the scarred and rugged mountains frown upon us again, and for hours we wind along their sides, looking down upon a tumbling river, its waters sometimes almost within our reach and sometimes lost below. We suddenly cross the deep black gorge of the Fraser River on

THE OLYMPIAN MTS. FROM THE GOVERNOR'S HOUSE, VANCOUVER ISLAND.   BY H.R.H. PRINCESS LOUISE.

a massive bridge of steel, seemingly constructed in mid-air, plunge through a tunnel, and enter the famous cañon of the Fraser.

The view here changes from the grand to the terrible. Through this gorge, so deep and narrow in many places that the rays of the sun hardly enter it, the black and ferocious waters of the great river force their way. We are in the heart of the Cascade range, and above the walls of the cañon we occasionally see the mountain peaks gleaming against the sky. Hundreds of feet above the river is the railway, notched into the face of the cliffs, now and then crossing a great chasm by a tall viaduct or disappearing in a tunnel through a projecting spur of rock, but so well made, and so thoroughly protected everywhere, that we feel no sense of danger. For hours we are deafened by the roar of the waters below, and we pray for the broad sunshine once more. The scene is fascinating in its terror, and we finally leave it gladly, yet regretfully.

At Yale the cañon ends and the river widens out, but we have mountains yet in plenty, at times receding and then drawing near again. We see Chinamen washing gold on the sand-bars and Indians herding cattle in the meadows; and the villages of the Indians, each with its little unpainted houses and miniature chapel, alternate rapidly with the collection of huts where the Chinamen congregate. Salmon drying on poles near the river give brilliant touches of colour to the landscape, and here and there we see the curious graveyards of the Indians, neatly enclosed and decorated with banners, streamers, and all manner of carved "totems."

A gleaming white cone rises towards the southeast. It is Mount Baker, sixty miles away and fourteen thousand feet above us. We cross large rivers flowing into the Fraser, all moving slowly here as if resting after their tumultuous passage down between the mountain ranges. As the valley widens out farms and orchards become more and more frequent, and our hearts are gladdened with the sight of broom and gorse and other shrubs and plants familiar to English eyes, for as we approach the coast we find a climate like that of the south of England, but with more sunshine. Touching the Fraser River now and then, we see an occasional steamboat, and here in the lower part the water is dotted with Indian canoes, all engaged in catching salmon, which visit these rivers in astonishing numbers, and which when caught are frozen and sent eastward by the railway, or canned in great quantities and shipped to all parts of the world.

Passing through a forest of mammoth trees, some of them twelve feet or more in diameter, and nearly three hundred feet high, we find ourselves on the

HOTEL VANCOUVER, VANCOUVER, BRITISH COLUMBIA.

tidewaters of the Pacific at the eastern extremity of Burrard Inlet. Following down the shore of this mountain-girt inlet for half an hour, our train rolls into the station at Vancouver, the western terminus of the Canadian Pacific Railway.

E soon find comfortable quarters in a fine hotel, equal to any we have seen in the East, and its situation on high ground affords us a most interesting and charming view of the new city, and the surrounding country. Far away at the southeast Mount Baker looms up all white and serene. At the north, and rising directly from the sea, is a beautiful group of the Cascade Mountains, bathed in a violet light and vividly reflected in the glassy waters of the inlet. Looking towards the west, out over English Bay and the Straits of Georgia, we see the dark-blue mountains of Vancouver Island, and at the southwest, beyond the broad delta of Fraser River, is the Olympian range,—a long line of opalescent peaks fading into the distance.

At our feet is a busy scene. The city is new indeed; only one or two of its many buildings were here two years ago,—a forest stood here then. The men who built the town could not wait for bricks and mortar, and all of the earlier houses were built of wood; but now many solid handsome structures of brick and stone are going up, and there is more of a come-to-stay look about it all. Down at the water's edge are long wharves where steamships from China and Japan, from California, Puget Sound and Alaska, are discharging or taking in cargoes; and at the warehouses along the wharves are lines of railway cars loading for the east with teas, silks, seal-skins, fish, fruit and many other commodities. Here and there all around the inlet, are great saw-mills, where steamships and sailing vessels are taking in timber and deals for China and Australia, and even for England. A few miles away is New Westminister, on the Fraser, one of the old towns of British Columbia, now quickened into vigorous growth by the advent of the railway, and the columns of smoke rising in that direction tell us of its extensive salmon canneries and saw-mills. There, too, ships are loading for all parts of the world. And over against Vancouver Island are other columns of smoke, indicating

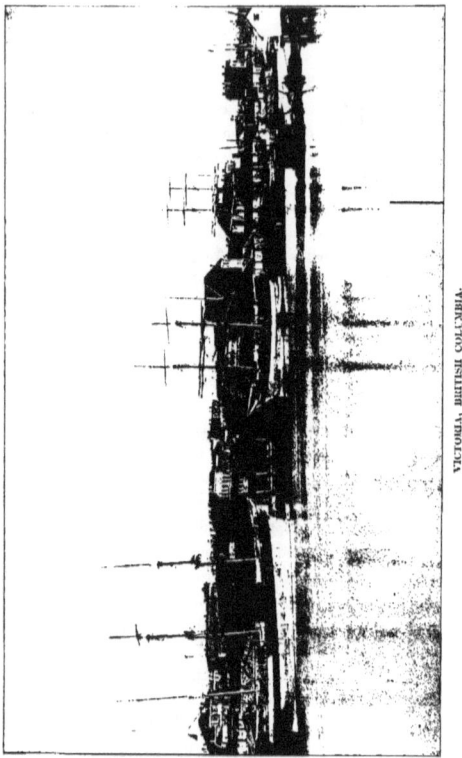

VICTORIA, BRITISH COLUMBIA.

the great coal mines from which nearly all of the steamships of the Pacific are supplied.

Northward for twelve hundred miles through the Gulf of Georgia and the wonderful fiords of Alaska, where the mountains are embraced in a thousand arms of the sea, pleasure-steamers, crowded with tourists, ply frequently. Southwestward the Straits of Fuca lead out past the entrance to Puget Sound and past the city of Victoria, to the open Pacific. All these waters, from Puget Sound to Alaska, hardly known a few years ago, are now dotted with all kinds of craft, from the largest to the smallest, engaged in all manner of trade.

No wonder that with all her magnificent resources in precious metals, her coal and iron, her inexhaustible fisheries and vast forests, her delightful climate and rich valleys, her matchless harbours and her newly completed transcontinental railway, British Columbia expects a brilliant future; and no wonder that everybody here is at work with all his might!

I ask your pardon, patient reader, for my persistence in showing you all sorts of things as we came along, whether you wished to see them or not. My anxiety that you should miss nothing you might wish to see is my only excuse. You have been bored nearly to death, no doubt, and I have noticed signs of impatience which lead me to suspect your desire for freedom to go and see as you like, and as you have found that no guide is necessary, I will, with your permission, leave you here; but before releasing your hand, let me advise you not to fail, now that you are so near, to visit Victoria, the beautiful capital of British Columbia. A steamer will take you there in a few hours, and you will be rewarded in finding a transplanted section of Old England, climate, people and all; and more vigourous, perhaps, because of the transplanting. Near Victoria you will find Esquimalt, the North Pacific naval station, and an iron-clad or two, and perchance some old friends from home; and let me advise you, furthermore, to take all of your luggage with you to Victoria, for I am sure you will be in no hurry to come away.

THE CANADIAN PACIFIC RAILWAY.

THE IMPERIAL HIGHWAY FROM THE ATLANTIC TO THE PACIFIC.

The Newest, The Most Solidly Constructed and the Best Equipped Transcontinental Route.

PARTICULAR ATTENTION IS CALLED TO THE

PARLOR AND SLEEPING-CAR SERVICE,

So important an accessory upon a railway whose cars are run upwards of

THREE THOUSAND MILES

without change.

Interior View of Canadian Pacific Railway Sleeping Car.

These cars are of unusual strength and size, with berths, smoking and toilet accommodations correspondingly roomy. The transcontinental sleeping-cars are provided with

BATH ROOMS,

and all are fitted with double doors and windows to exclude the dust in summer and the cold in winter.

The seats are richly upholstered, with high backs and arms, and the central sections are made into luxurious sofas during the day.

The upper berths are provided with windows and ventilators, and have curtains separate from those of the berths beneath. The exteriors are of polished red mahogany, and the interiors are of white mahogany and satinwood, elaborately carved; while the lamps, brackets, berth-locks, and other pieces of metal work, are of old brass of antique design.

THE FIRST-CLASS DAY COACHES are proportionately elaborate in their arrangement for the comfort of the passenger; and, for those who desire to travel at a cheaper rate, *COLONIST SLEEPING CARS* are provided without additional charge. These cars are fitted with upper and lower berths after the same general style as other sleeping-cars, but are not upholstered, and the passenger may furnish his own bedding, or purchase it of the Company's agents at terminal stations at nominal rates. The entire passenger equipment is *matchless* in elegance and comfort.

FIRST-CLASS SLEEPING AND PARLOR CAR TARIFF.

FOR ONE LOWER OR ONE UPPER BERTH IN SLEEPING CAR BETWEEN

Quebec and Montreal.....$1.50	Pt. Arthur & Vancouver.$15.00	Boston and Montreal......$2.00
Montreal and Toronto......2.00	Toronto and Chicago......3.00	New York and Montreal....2.00
Montreal and Winnipeg....8.00	Toronto and Detroit......2.00	Chicago and St. Paul.....2.00
Montreal and Vancouver...20.00	Toronto and Winnipeg......8.00	St. Paul and Winnipeg.....3.00
Ottawa and Toronto........2.00	Toronto and Vancouver...18.50	St. Paul and Vancouver...13.50
Ottawa and Vancouver ...20.00		Winnipeg and Vancouver..12.00

FOR ONE SEAT IN PARLOR CAR BETWEEN

Quebec and Montreal......$0.75	Montreal and Toronto.....$1.00	Toronto and Owen Sound.$0.50
Three Rivers and Montreal .50	Ottawa and Toronto.......1.00	Toronto and St. Thomas.... .50
Montreal and Ottawa...... .50	Peterboro' and Toronto..... .95	Toronto and Detroit.........1.00

Between other stations rates are in proportion. Accommodation in First-Class Sleeping Cars and in Parlor Cars will be sold only to holders of First-Class transportation.

THE CANADIAN PACIFIC RAILWAY
DINING CARS
Excel in Elegance of Design and Furniture

AND IN THE

Quality of Food and Attendance

ANYTHING HITHERTO OFFERED TO

TRANSCONTINENTAL TRAVELLERS.

The fare provided is the best procurable, and the cooking has a wide reputation for excellence. Local delicacies, such as trout, prairie hens, antelope steaks, Fraser River salmon, succeed one another as the train moves westward.

The wines are of the Company's special importation, and are of the finest quality.

These cars accompany all transcontinental trains, and are managed directly by the Railway Company, which seeks, as with its hotels and sleeping cars, to provide every comfort and luxury without regard to cost—looking to the general profit of the Railway rather than to the immediate returns from these branches of its service

47

₵ANADIAN ₱ACIFIC ₦OTELS

While the perfect sleeping and dining-car service, peculiar to the Canadian Pacific Railway, provides every comfort and luxury for travellers making the continuous trip between the Atlantic and Pacific coasts, the Railway was no sooner opened than it was found necessary to provide places at the principal points of interest among the mountains, where tourists and others might explore and enjoy, at their leisure, the magnificent scenery with which the line abounds.

With this end in view, the Company have erected at convenient points, hotels which will not only serve these purposes, but should, by their special excellence, add another to the many elements of superiority for which the Railway is already famous.

Proceeding westward, the first point selected was Banff, about twenty miles within the Rocky Mountains and forty miles east of their summit, where the natural attractions of the place had already led the Government to set aside an extensive tract as a National Park.

THE BANFF SPRINGS HOTEL

is placed on a high mountain promontory, 4,500 feet above the sea level, at the confluence of the Bow and Spray rivers, and is a large, handsome and well-built structure, with every convenience that modern ingenuity can suggest, and costing about a quarter of a million dollars. While it is not intended to be a sanitarium, in the usual sense, the needs and comforts of invalids are fully provided for, and the hotel will be kept open throughout the year. The hot sulphur springs, with which the region abounds, vary in temperature from 80 to 121 degrees, and in addition to the bathing facilities provided by the hotel, the Government has protected, improved and beautified the springs, and constructed picturesque bathing-houses and swimming baths. The springs are much like those of Arkansas, and the apparently greater curative properties of the waters are no doubt due, in part, to the cool, dry air of the mountains incident to their elevation, The spring waters are specially efficacious for the cure of rheumatic, gouty and allied affections, and are very beneficial in affections of the liver, diabetes, Bright's disease and chronic dyspepsia.

A number of sub-ranges of the Rocky Mountains radiate from Banff, and looking up the valleys between them, in every direction, long lines of white peaks are seen in grand perspective. A dozen mountain monarchs within view raise their heads a mile or more above the hotel ; and the Bow River, coming down from its glacier sources at the west, widens out as it approaches, then suddenly contracts and plunges over a precipice immediately at our feet, and then widening out again, is finally lost among the snow-capped peaks toward the east.

Mountain sheep and goats abound in the neighboring hills, and Devil's Head Lake, not far away, a deep glacier-fed body of water, a mile or two in width, and fifteen miles long, affords excellent sport in deep trolling for trout, which are here taken of extraordinary size.

The hotel rates are from $3.50 per day and upwards, according to the rooms selected, and special rates by the week or the month will be given on application to

GEORGE HOLLIDAY, Manager,

Banff, Alberta, N.W.T., Canada

THE MOUNT STEPHEN HOUSE,

a pretty chalet-like hotel, is situated fifty miles west of Banff, in Kicking Horse Cañon, at the base of Mount Stephen,— the chief peak of the Rockies in this latitude, whose stupendous mass is lifted abruptly 8,000 feet above. This is a favorite stopping-place for tourists and mountain climbers, and there is good fly fishing for trout in a pretty lake near by, and "big horns" and mountain goats are found in the vicinity. Looking down the valley from the hotel, the Ottertail Mountains are seen on the left, and the Van Horne range on the right. In the latter, the two most prominent peaks are Mts. Deville and King. This is a favorite region for artists, the lights and shadows on the near and distant mountains giving especially interesting subjects for the brush.

The hotel is noted for the excellence of its cuisine, and is fitted up with every attention to comfort.

The rates are three dollars per day, and for the engagement of special accommodation, application should be made to   JAS. WHARTON, Manager,
Field, B. C., Canada.

GLACIER HOUSE,

the next resting-place, is situated in the heart of the Selkirks, at the foot of " Sir Donald," and in close proximity to the Great Glacier—a sea of ice spreading among the mountains, and covering an area of about thirty-eight square miles.

The hotel is built beside the railway, in a beautiful amphitheatre surrounded by lofty mountains, of which Sir Donald, rising 8,000 feet above the railway, is the most prominent. Northward stand the summit peaks of the Selkirks in grand array, all clad in snow and ice, and westward is the deep valley of the glacier-fed Illicilliwaet River, leading away to its junction with the Columbia. The dense forests all about are filled with the music of restless brooks, which will irresistibly attract the trout fisherman, and the hunter for large game can have his choice of "big horns," mountain goats, grizzly and mountain bears. The main point of interest is the Great Glacier, which is only a short walk from the hotel by a pleasant and easy path. One may safely climb upon its wrinkled surface, or penetrate its water-worn caves, and think himself in grottos carved in emerald or sapphire. The glacier is about five hundred feet thick at its forefoot, and is said to exceed in area all the glaciers of Switzerland combined.

No tourist should fail to stop here for a day at least, and he need not be surprised to find himself loth to leave its attractions at the end of a week or month.

The hotel is similar in construction to the Mount Stephen House, and is first-class in all respects. The rates are three dollars per day, and correspondence should be addressed to
H. A. PERLY, Manager,
Glacier House, British Columbia.

THE FRASER CAÑON HOUSE,

(rates three dollars per day, E. J. ERMATINGER, Manager), at North Bend, 130 miles east of Vancouver, is situated in a park-like opening among the mountains on the Fraser River; its construction is of the Swiss chalet style, similar to the Mount Stephen and Glacier Houses, and it is managed with the same attention to the comfort of its patrons that pervades all branches of the Company's service. The scenery all along the Fraser River is not only interesting, but startling. It has been well described as "ferocious," and the hotel is a comfortable base from which to explore the surrounding mountains and valleys.

HOTEL VANCOUVER,

at Vancouver, B.C., the Pacific coast terminus of the Railway. The Company have just completed this magnificent hotel, designed to accommodate the large commercial business of the place, as well as the great number of tourists who will always find it profitable and interesting to make here a stop of a day or two, whether travelling east or west. It is situated on high ground near the centre of the city, and from it there is a glorious outlook in every direction. No effort has been spared in making its accommodations and service perfect in every detail, and in the matters of cuisine, furnishings and sanitary arrangements it will compare favorably with the best hotels in eastern Canada or the United States.

Rates: three to five dollars per day, with special terms for a longer time.
E. M. MATTHEWS, Manager,
Vancouver, B. C.

DRIARD HOUSE,

Victoria, B. C. This hotel is so well known by all travellers to the North Pacific coast as to require but little description in these pages. Its ownership and management are not connected with the Railway, and all communications should be addressed to Messrs. HARTNAGLE & REDON, Managers. The house is large and well furnished, having undergone recent alterations and improvements, and it is conveniently situated near the business centre of the city. The special elegance of its table d'hote has made the house widely famous.

GENERAL OFFICERS CANADIAN PACIFIC RAILWAY.

HEAD OFFICES: MONTREAL, CANADA.

W. C. Van Horne ....President..Montreal.
Charles Drinkwater ....Secretary.. "
T. G. Shaughnessy.......Assistant General Manager........................ "
George Olds............General Traffic Manager........................... "
Lucius Tuttle ....Passenger Traffic Manager......................... "
Henry Beatty..........Manager Steamship Lines and Lake Traffic..........Toronto.
I. G. Ogden............Comptroller.......................................Montreal
W. Sutherland Taylor..Treasurer.. "
L. A. Hamilton.........Land Commissioner.................................Winnipeg.
Wm. Whyte.............General Superintendent, Western Division........... "
Harry Abbott.........General Superintendent, Pacific Division...........Vancouver.
C. W. Spencer.........General Superintendent, Eastern Division..........Montreal.
T. A. Mackinnon.......General Superintendent, Ontario & Atlantic Division..... "
Robert Kerr..........General Freight and Passenger Agent, W. & P. Divs..Winnipeg.
D. McNicoll...........Gen'l Pass'r Agent, Ontario & Atlantic and Eastern Divs..Montreal.
G. M. Bosworth........Asst. Freight Traffic Manager, Ont. & Atl. and East. Divs. "
J. N. Sutherland .....General Freight Agent, Ontario Division............Toronto.
J. A. Sheffield ......Superintendent Dining, Sleeping and Parlor Cars....Montreal.
E. S. Anderson........General Baggage Agent.............................. "

AGENCIES:

Adelaide.......So. Aus...Agents Oceanic Steamship Co.................
Boston ....Mass.{ C. E. McPherson, District Passenger Agent... }211 Washington St.
                       { H. J. Colvin, City Passenger Agent.......... }
Brockville........Ont...A. Caswell, Ticket Agent.......................145 Main Street.
Buffalo...........N.Y...Walter Hurd, Ticket Agent......................15 Exchange Street.
Chicago............Ill..J. Francis Lee, Commercial Agent..............232 So. Clark St.
Glasgow ......Scotland..Archer Baker, European Traffic Agent..........135 Buchanan St.
Halifax...........N.S...C. R. Barry, Ticket Agent......................126 Hollis Street.
Hamilton..........Ont...W. J. Grant ....8 James Street, So.
Hong Kong......China...Messrs. Adamson, Bell & Co., Agents for China.
Liverpool..........Eng..Archer Baker, European Traffic Agent..........17 James Street.
London.............Eng..Archer Baker, European Traffic Agent..........88 Cannon Street.
London.............Eng..T. R. Parker, Ticket Agent.....................Richmond Street.
Montreal ....Que..A. B. Chaffee, Jr., City Passenger Agent.......266 St. James St.
                      { E. V. Skinner, General Eastern Agent..........387 Broadway.
New York.........N.Y.{ J. Ottenhelmer, Land and Emigration Agent......30 State Street.
                      { Everett Frazar, China and Japan Agent.........124 Water Street.
Niagara Falls ....N.Y..D. Isaacs ....Prospect House.
Niagara Falls......Out..George M. Colburn..............................Clifton House.
Ottawa............Ont...J. E. Parker, City Passenger Agent ....42 Sparks Street.
Philadelphia ......Pa...H. McMurtrie....................................Cor.3d & Chestn't St.
Portland...........Me...M. L. Williams.................................Port. & Ogdens. R.R.
Portland..........Ore..C. G. McCord, Freight and Passenger Agent......6 Washington St.
Quebec...........Que...J. W. Ryder, City Passenger Agent ....St. Louis Hotel.
St. John..........N.B...Messrs. Chubb & Co., Ticket Agents ....
                      { Messrs. Goodall, Perkins & Co., Agts. Pac. Coast }10 Market Street.
San Francisco.....Cal.{ Steamship Co ....}
                      { D. B. Jackson, Passenger Agent ....214 Montgomery St.
                      { M. M. Stern, Passenger Agent...................222 Montgomery St.
Seattle.....Wash. Ter...E. W. MacGinnes, Freight and Passenger Agent.
Shanghai........China...Messrs. Adamson, Bell & Co., Agents for China.
Sydney..........N.S.W...Alex. Woods, Agent for Australia..............
Tacoma.......Wash. Ter...E. E. Ellis, Freight and Passenger Agent......
Toronto...........Ont...W. R. Callaway, District Passenger Agent......110 King Street, W.
Vancouver.........B.C...D. E. Brown, Dis. Freight and Passenger Agent.
Victoria..........B.C...Rob't Irving, Freight and Passenger Agent.....Government Street.
Winnipeg.........Man...G. H. Campbell, City Ticket Agent..............471 Main Street.
Yokohama.......Japan...Messrs. Frazar & Co., Agents for Japan........

A List of Tours over the Canadian Pacific Railway

will be forwarded to any address on application to the Company's Agencies
at London or Liverpool, Eng., New York, Boston and Chicago,
or to the Passenger Traffic Manager at Montreal.